To the loves of my life ... Andrew, Riley, Kayleigh & Nolan
—KCB

Text Copyright © 2020 Keri Claiborne Boyle
Illustration Copyright © 2020 Daniel Duncan
Design Copyright © 2020 Sleeping Bear Press

All inquiries should be addressed to: Sleeping Bear Press
2395 South Huron Parkway, Suite 200, Ann Arbor, MI 48104
www.sleepingbearpress.com
© Sleeping Bear Press

Printed and bound in China.
10 9 8 7 6 5 4 3 2 1
Library of Congress Cataloging-in-Publication Data
Names: Boyle, Keri, author. | Duncan, Daniel, illustrator.
Title: Otis P. Oliver protests / by Keri Claiborne Boyle ; illustrated by Daniel Duncan.
Description: Ann Arbor, MI : Sleeping Bear Press, [2020] | Audience: Ages 4–8.
Summary: Otis P. Oliver rouses a rabble of neighborhood children
to join him in a protest demonstration against baths, but notes from his
mother, conveyed by his sisters, lead to a compromise.
Identifiers: LCCN 2019047091 | ISBN 9781534110434 (hardcover)
Subjects: CYAC: Baths--Fiction. | Family life--Fiction. | Humorous stories.
Classification: LCC PZ7.1.B7 Oti 2020 | DDC [E]--dc23
LC record available at https://lccn.loc.gov/2019047091

Otis P. Oliver Protests

by Keri Claiborne Boyle and Illustrated by Daniel Duncan

Published by Sleeping Bear Press

Otis P. Oliver
refused to take a bath.

If it were up to him, baths would be strictly prohibited.
However, when you have an **oldest** big sister,

a **middle** big sister,

and a **youngest** big sister,

your opinions tend to be equal
to that of the family dog.

It's worth mentioning that the dog only gets one bath a month.
Otis gets four baths a *week*, especially when he's excessively grubby.

And since worm farms aren't going to build themselves,
Otis is usually excessively grubby.

Now, every time he came near,
his family held their noses.

This meant Otis's anti-bath stance would likely result in a **tense** family standoff.

To avoid the tub, he'd need to be taken seriously.
But being taken seriously required a more serious look.

He'd also need backup—so Otis rounded up his neighborhood pals
and delivered a fiery speech.

"We must unite!
Fight the establishment! Demand bath-time rights!
The only thing we have to fear is soap itself!"

Then they marched all the way up Snickerdoodle Street,
attracting attention as they went.

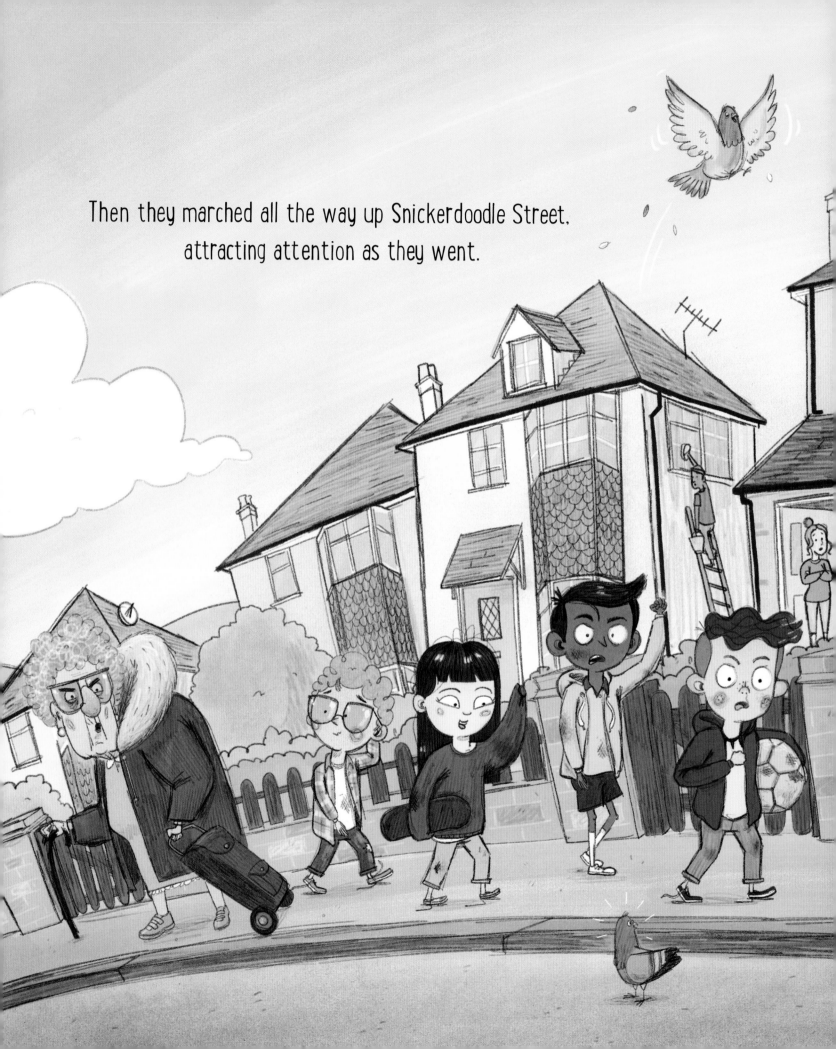

Next, Otis led the unruly crowd to picket the driveway.

Finally, the crew plopped down in Otis's front yard—
refusing to move until certain demands were met.

After some time, the front door opened and Otis's **oldest** big sister stomped across the yard and thrust a note at him.

He turned the note over and scratched out a quick response.

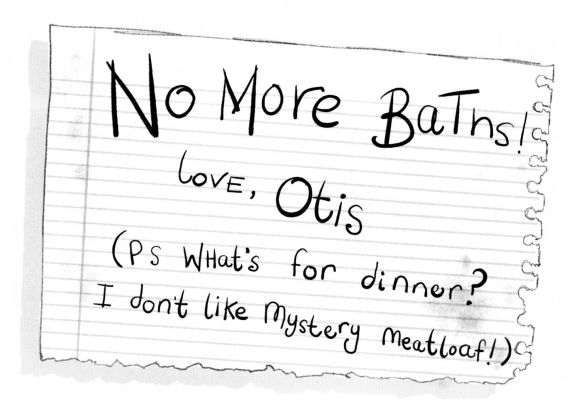

He handed it to his sister, who snorted and stomped back into the house.

Five minutes later, his **middle** big sister came out and, with a hand on one hip and a loud sigh, dropped a second note into Otis's lap.

Sweetheart: Why don't you want to take a bath?
— Love, Mom x

(PS don't worry...
        it's lasagna night)

Otis scribbled another reply.

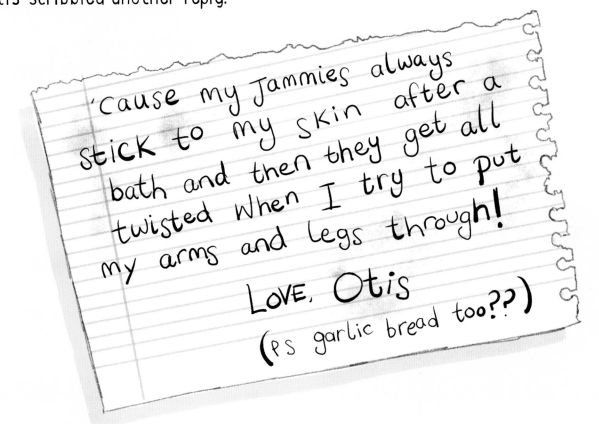

'cause my jammies always stick to my skin after a bath and then they get all twisted when I try to put my arms and legs through!

LOVE, Otis

(PS garlic bread too??)

He gave it to his sister, who rolled her eyes and sauntered off.

Five minutes after that, the door opened yet again,
and out skipped his tutu-wearing **youngest** big sister,
who performed a quick pirouette before handing Otis another note.

Oh, dear. That is a problem.
What if jammies were optional
from now on? You can always
just wear your birthday suit.
              All my love, Mom
(PS of course there's garlic bread!)

Otis mulled over his mom's response.
Then he huddled with his closest supporters to discuss the offer.
Finally, he jotted down his answer.

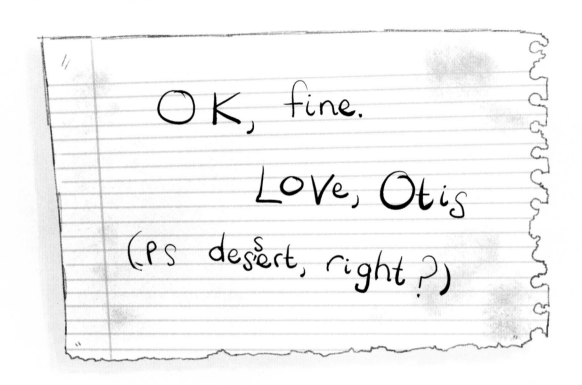

OK, fine.

Love, Otis

(PS desert, right?)

He handed it to his sister, who twirled away.

But then, as Otis stood up, thanked his fellow protesters, and sent them on their way, the dog padded out with a slobbery note in her mouth. Otis grabbed it.

My lil grub worm,
So glad we reached a compromise.
Now get in the tub before you're
grounded for life!

Hugs and kisses, Mom x
(PS No dessert on school nights)

Otis headed inside, ready to hop in the tub.

Maybe he'd leave a *little* smudge somewhere,

just for old times' sake.

But first,
there was one last thing
he needed to do.

Dear Mom,

Happy to announce I'll take a bath, but NO soap! Maybe if there was dessert tonight, I'd consider a compromise.

Much love, Otis

(P.s Ice cream—preferably chocolate)

SOAP